About the Author

Jennifer Susanne Mottley is a single mother to two children. She studied at Middlesex University and achieved a BA honours degree in religious studies. She was nine years old when she first began to write stories.

She also enjoys knitting, sports and church activities.

A Pet for Bronwyn

J. S. Mottley

A Pet for Bronwyn

Olympia Publishers
London

www.olympiapublishers.com
OLYMPIA PAPERBACK EDITION

A CIP catalogue record for this title is
available from the British Library.

ISBN: 978-1-78830-230-2

First Published in 2019

Olympia Publishers
60 Cannon Street
London
EC4N 6NP

Printed in Great Britain

Dedication

I would like to dedicate my book to Mr Frederick Finney who was my Head Teacher at Woodlands Junior School. He gave me inspiration and encouragement and support when he discovered that I liked writing.

Acknowledgments

I would like to acknowledge my friends and family for all their kind words and faith in me. I am grateful for all their generosity.

Bronwyn loved animals. She liked going to the park to feed the ducks with her oldest sister Georgette. She enjoyed watching the ducks and ducklings swimming in the lake.

If there were any television programmes about animals, Bronwyn liked to watch them. She enjoyed the safari programmes, especially the ones about big cats. None of her siblings were very interested in these types of programmes, so Bronwyn often watched them alone.

One day, Mummy and Daddy decided to take the children to an aquarium. It was the summer holidays and they had just come back from a holiday in Southampton. They had been to see their Uncle Raymond and Aunty Mary, who had a big double fronted house out in the Southampton suburbs. The children had thought the house was beautiful, more so than their own. Now they were home again in East London. Mummy felt it would be good to spend the rest of the six weeks' holidays going on day trips. The aquarium seemed like a good idea.

Bronwyn, Michelle, Georgette, Barack and Herbert went by bus and train to the aquarium, with Mummy and Daddy. It was fun sitting by the window and watching all the houses and shops as they went by.

When they arrived at the aquarium, they had to queue to get in. There were lots of people outside. Apparently, they all had the same idea; to visit the aquarium. There was a special family ticket which could be bought to save money. Mummy and Daddy decided that buying it was the best option.

Barack was rather impatient in the queue but Mr and Mrs Cedar told him that it would not take long.

"There are sometimes delays on aeroplanes as well," Mr Cedar reminded Barack. Mr Cedar was an airline pilot. "I have to get used to delays myself."

Barack did not feel he wanted to be a pilot when he grew up. He knew his sister Georgette wanted to be one though.

At last they were in the aquarium. Barack immediately began to draw pictures and sketches of all the beautiful fish and sea life. He had brought his painting set with him. Drawing was one of Barack's hobbies.

After they had looked around the aquarium, they went into the restaurant for lunch. There were sandwiches, cakes, crisps, fruit and other food behind the safety glass at the counter. They all decided to have jacket potatoes for lunch. The fillings varied; cheese, baked beans, butter, chilli con carne, ham and chicken curry.

When it was time to go home, Bronwyn was very upset about leaving the aquarium and Mrs Cedar knew Bronwyn loved animals, so she suggested that on the way home they would go to the local pet shop.

When they got to the pet shop, Bronwyn expressed a preference for a rabbit. So Mummy and Daddy bought one for her. They also bought food for the rabbit and arranged to have the pet rabbit's hutch delivered to their house.

Barack, Herbert, Georgette, and Michelle decided on a name for Bronwyn's pet rabbit. They chose to call the rabbit "Biscuits". Bronwyn was happy with the name as she was indecisive about choosing one herself.

Biscuits' hutch was put in the conservatory. It was clean, dry and cool. The hutch had been delivered in the evening on the same day that they had chosen Biscuits the rabbit, so the children were able to make it comfortable for Biscuits to sleep in.

Bronwyn adored Biscuits. She played and played with her all day long. She fed Biscuits out in the garden and watched as Biscuits ran around and chased the birds.

The other children, Barack, Herbert, Michelle and Georgette, although they were not as keen on animals as their little sister, Bronwyn was, still began to grow fond of little Biscuits, Bronwyn's pet rabbit.

Mr and Mrs Cedar made sure that Biscuits had plenty of food, water and also fresh straw for the cage, and fresh air as well.

Sometimes Biscuits went into the garden for exercise by herself. The children filmed her on Daddy's old-fashioned camcorder.

Bronwyn was very happy with her pet rabbit. She wondered how she had ever coped without her. The children attended youth church most weeks, and occasionally there would be a service especially for animals. Bronwyn decided that when the church put on another special service for pets again, she would definitely take Biscuits along. As for Biscuits, she did not seem to mind at all.